Lincoln School Library

HALLUCINOGENS

Hallucinogens twist the way users see the world around them.

THE DRUG ABUSE PREVENTION LIBRARY

HALLUCINOGENS

Ann Ricki Hurwitz
Sue Hurwitz

THE ROSEN PUBLISHING GROUP, INC.
NEW YORK

Published in 1992, 1996, 1999 by The Rosen Publishing Group, Inc.
29 East 21st Street, New York, NY 10010

Revised Edition 1999

Library of Congress Cataloging-in-Publication Data

Hurwitz, Ann Ricki
    Hallucinogens / by Ann Ricki Hurwitz and Sue Hurwitz.—rev. ed.
       p.   cm.—(The Drug abuse prevention library)
    Includes bibliographical references and index.
    Summary: Describes psilocybin, LSD, mescaline, and other hallucinogenic drugs and discusses their dangerous and destructive effects.
    ISBN 0-8239-3006-8
    1. Hallucinogenic drugs—Juvenile literature. 2. [1. Hallucinogenic drugs. 2. Drugs. 3. Drug abuse.] I. Hurwitz, Ann Ricki. II. Title. III. Series.
    HV5809.5.H87 1999
    362.29'4—dc20   92-8599
                                       CIP
                                       AC

Manufactured in the United States of America

Contents

Introduction

Illiana and Lara had decided to ditch their last-period class to hang out with the guys by the basketball courts. They were having a great time when Peter took out a joint and passed it around. Lara took a long hit. Illiana didn't really want to smoke it, but she didn't want to look like a baby either, so she took a puff.

On her way home, Illiana started to feel queasy. The next morning her stomach still hurt, and her head was pounding. Illiana knew the marijuana had made her sick, and she never touched another joint again.

Hallucinogens are among the oldest drugs used by humans. These drugs cause users to hallucinate—to hear or see things that are not there. For centuries, naturally occurring hallucinogens such as mescaline, peyote, "magic mushrooms," and marijuana have been used for medical, social, and religious purposes. More recently, synthetic versions of hallucinogenic drugs have been produced, such as PCP, LSD, ecstasy, and "Special K."

Many people think that the abuse of hallucinogens was a problem only in the 1960s, but the truth is that hallucinogen use today is on the rise, particularly among teens. According to a 1998 study, 49 percent of twelfth graders—that's almost half—have tried marijuana.

Hallucinogen use is both illegal and very dangerous. These drugs change users' perceptions of reality, making them act in unpredictable and often unsafe ways. Hallucinogens can also be addictive.

Some teens turn to drugs as a way to cope with the demands of family, school, and friends. What these teens don't know is that drugs will not help and may even create more problems. The most important thing to realize is that teens can overcome their problems without drugs. This book will discuss the many dangers associated with hallucinogens and where to find help if you or someone you know has a problem with them.

Many hallucinogens are made from plants like the peyote cactus.

CHAPTER 1

Hallucinogens— What They Are and What They Do

*T*here are many kinds of drugs. Some are legal and are used to help cure illnesses. Some are illegal and can only harm people. Some drugs are natural; that is, they occur in the world. They are plants, or parts of plants. Other drugs are human-made. They are made in laboratories by scientists. Some human-made drugs are legal and useful. Others are illegal and very dangerous. Hallucinogens fall into the illegal-and-dangerous category.

10 | ## *Natural Hallucinogens*

Magic Mushrooms

Mushrooms are plants called *fungi*. Fungi live on living or dead plants. Mushrooms grow all around the world. There are thousands of kinds of mushrooms. The kind that you find in grocery stores are safe and are also good for you.

But some mushrooms are poisonous and can kill you. Some mushrooms—called magic mushrooms—contain a chemical called *psilocybin*. This natural chemical is a hallucinogen.

Magic mushrooms may be eaten fresh, cooked, dried, or crushed. Usually they are swallowed in tablets or capsules.

The psilocybin in magic mushrooms causes users to see, hear, and feel things in ways that are not normal. Often users see very colorful hallucinations. They may feel light-headed or so relaxed that nothing seems to matter. Psilocybin may also cause diarrhea and stomach cramps.

The effects of magic mushrooms begin in about 15 minutes and may last 9 hours. Sometimes users have flashbacks.

Mescaline

Peyote is a short, spineless cactus plant. It grows in the deserts of Mexico and the southwestern United States. The top of the cactus has a little crown or button. This button contains a chemical called *mescaline*.

Slices of the peyote crown may be eaten fresh or dried into hard, brown buttons. The buttons are often swallowed whole or used to make tea. Peyote buttons can be kept for many years.

Mescaline can also be made by humans. Human-made mescaline is most often found in capsules or tablets.

Mescaline changes the way the brain works. It causes users to see things, especially colors, that are not real. Mescaline can cause hallucinations.

About an hour after using mescaline, trippers may have physical effects such as nausea and vomiting. They may have ragged breathing, increased heart rate, or the shakes. Sometimes the pupils of the eyes are dilated, or enlarged. The effects of mescaline have been known to last up to 12 hours.

Mescaline, or peyote, has been known as a mind-changing drug for hundreds of years. The Aztecs of South America used peyote in religious ceremonies. Even today some Native Americans want to use it in their religious ceremonies.

12 | Marijuana

Marijuana is sometimes called "pot" or "grass." Marijuana is a drug made from the cannabis, or hemp, plant. This plant grows in warm climates all over the world, including the United States.

The cannabis plant contains more than 400 chemicals. Many of the chemicals stay in a user's body for months. *Tetrahydrocannabinol*, or THC, is the chemical in marijuana that is a hallucinogen.

Marijuana may be added to food or brewed into tea. Usually it is smoked in handmade cigarettes called "joints," "sticks," or "reefers." Smoking one joint of marijuana is as harmful as smoking five cigarettes made of tobacco.

Marijuana may injure both the body and the mind. When smoking marijuana, the tripper holds in the smoke as long as possible. That is very harmful to the lungs. Long-term use may cause lung cancer and heart disease. Marijuana is harmful to the white blood cells, which help fight off disease. Many users become sick more often than nonusers.

Marijuana changes the way the brain works. The effects of marijuana begin about 15 to 30 minutes after using it.

Many people suffer serious side effects from taking drugs.

14 Users may feel relaxed, drowsy, or happy. They may have mild hallucinations for several hours. When that happens the user is said to be "high," or "stoned."

Some users find it hard to think clearly or remember things. They may become moody, easily upset, or unable to pay attention. They may talk and giggle more than usual. That makes it hard for them to learn at school or on the job. Sometimes they have panic reactions and feel that their lives are spinning out of control.

Drugs do not affect everyone the same way. Doctors still do not know all of the long-term effects of using marijuana. But doctors do know that longtime users of marijuana often become dependent on it. They need more and more marijuana just to feel normal.

Long-term marijuana use damages the brain and nervous system. Users may never think in a normal way again.

Human-Made Hallucinogens
LSD

LSD (*lysergic acid diethylamide*), commonly called "acid," is the most powerful known hallucinogen and can have some very serious effects on the body. In nature, LSD is found in a fungus that grows on rye and other grains. Most LSD used today is made synthetically. It is a colorless and odorless white powder, and it is most commonly found in tablet form or as a coating on sheets of special paper that are licked.

LSD can affect your body physically and mentally. The effects of LSD begin within thirty minutes and can last for up to twelve hours. It is impossible to predict how LSD will affect the body. It depends on the dosage, the user's mood, and what environment the user is in. Some LSD users report seeing bright colors, strange shapes, or religious images.

The following are some typical physical symptoms of LSD use:

- Trembling; "goose bumps"
- Nausea; headache; excessive sweating
- Raised body temperature and blood pressure; increased heart rate
- Extreme anxiety
- Irrational behavior

Since it is impossible to predict LSD's effects on the body, even longtime users sometimes have "bad trips." During a bad trip, a user experiences frightening hallucinations and may swing wildly between different emotions. She may feel confused or panicked. At times a user may be

16 convinced that she possesses superhuman strength. In this state she may try to do something dangerous or even deadly.

LSD is so powerful that its effects can remain in the body years after use. A one-time user can experience flashbacks decades after trying the drug. Flashbacks can be triggered by drug use or stress, but they can also happen without warning. In addition, female LSD users may be hurting their own children as well as themselves: some doctors think that LSD may harm babies born to users.

PCP

PCP, or *phencyclidine*, is the most dangerous hallucinogen. It is known and sold under as many as fifty different names, including "angel dust" and "wack."

In the 1950s PCP was used as a human anesthetic (something that numbs the body) until doctors discovered its dangerous side effects. It was used as an animal tranquilizer in the 1960s.

PCP can be swallowed, smoked, sniffed, or injected. Today PCP is mixed with many different ingredients. Depending on what else is added, its color can range from tan to brown, and it can be made into a powder, liquid, or gummy substance.

PCP can cause strange, violent behavior

The only sure way to avoid getting hooked on drugs is to refuse them.

18 and extreme mental confusion. Sometimes users think that they have superhuman powers and die from drowning, burns, falls from high places, or car accidents. Users high on PCP often commit violent crimes.

Many PCP users take overdoses and act crazy. Their eyes are jumpy and unfocused. They move like robots and seem spaced out. When that happens it is hard to tell a PCP user from a person who has serious mental problems.

This is because a person high on PCP really is mentally ill, even though his state may only be temporary. You can never be sure what the person may do. It is best to stay away from anyone on a PCP trip.

MDMA

MDMA, also called "ecstasy," is a "designer drug." Designer drugs are created by making small changes in the structure of an existing drug. The substances in some designer drugs are too new to have been listed as illegal under existing laws. It is still unlawful to create them, however, because of a 1986 law that makes it illegal to make, possess, or sell any drug that is chemically related to any illegal substance.

Ecstasy, like other designer drugs, is

often contaminated (mixed with other substances) or badly manufactured, since illegal labs can't hire trained chemists and often replace unavailable chemicals with other substances. For this reason, designer drugs are often more dangerous and powerful than the original drug.

Since ecstasy can distort users' perceptions of reality, it is considered a hallucinogen, but it also acts like a group of stimulants called amphetamines. Amphetamines, also called "speed" or "uppers," speed up the brain and body and make users feel alert.

For the first hour or so after use, many ecstasy users feel happy and outgoing. This rush is followed by calmness and an absence of worry. Ecstasy users also report heightened senses of touch, hearing, vision, taste, and smell.

Recently ecstasy has become very popular at "raves"—all-night underground parties—because it keeps users awake and energized throughout the night. But ecstasy can have many harmful effects. Besides hallucinations, this drug can cause panic and anxiety as well as nausea, blurred vision, and trembling. Also, like LSD, ecstasy can increase heart rate and blood pressure.

Hallucinogens can cause violent and unpredictable changes in mood.

In addition, distorted senses and
impaired judgment and coordination can
lead to serious accidents. And because
ecstasy prevents users from feeling pain,
people high on the drug can hurt themselves without even knowing it.

Special K

Special K (*ketamine hydrochloride*), one of
the newest street drugs, is also popular at
raves. Like PCP, ketamine is an animal
tranquilizer used by veterinarians. It is
also occasionally used on humans.

Ketamine can be snorted, mixed into
drinks, injected, or sprinkled on cigarettes
and smoked. Unfortunately veterinarians
don't always lock up the drug, so burglars
can access it easily.

Highs from Special K last between
thirty minutes and two hours and can
cause intense hallucinations and distorted
vision. The negative effects include
amnesia, potentially fatal breathing diffi-
culties, heart problems, and loss of bodily
coordination. Large doses can lead to
flashbacks and can also stop oxygen from
reaching the brain and muscles, which
can cause permanent damage or death.
Ketamine can also cause users to become
dependent on the drug.

21

Because drugs can change coordination and muscle control, users are more likely to cause serious accidents or injuries.

Some Dangers of Trying

*C*hanice was excited to be in New York City for the first time. She had saved up money for the trip for months. She was visiting some friends who promised to show her a great time, including a night out at one of the best nightclubs in the country. Chanice loved to dance to good music, and she was looking forward to the excitement and glamour of a club. Being only 17, she had never even gotten into a bar before. Her friends assured her that they would be able to get her into the club without her needing to show ID.

After a day of shopping and sightseeing, Chanice had dinner and got ready to go out. She and her friends Marvely

24 and Joanne first went to a couple of parties. They arrived at the club at 2:30 a.m. Chanice was already pretty tired, so Joanne suggested a "pick-me-up" before they hit the dance floor.

"Like what?" asked Chanice.

"Well, as long as you're here, you might as well have the full night-out treatment," said Joanne. "Would you like to try ecstasy?"

Chanice was uncertain, but curious. "What does it do?" she asked.

"You'll feel really happy and energetic, and you'll want to dance and hug people a lot," said Marvely. "Don't feel pressured. You don't have to do it, but we definitely are."

Chanice didn't want to be left out of the fun, and besides, she was feeling way too tired to dance. She felt she could use some energy. "Okay, why not? How much is it?" she asked.

"It's $25 a hit," said Joanne.

Ugh, thought Chanice, there goes $25 of my vacation money. Oh well, I really do want to dance.

She watched as Joanne approached a man in a baseball cap and baggy jeans who took her money and handed her three white capsules.

"I can't believe I'm doing this," Chanice said as she swallowed the capsule.

"Let's go sit down," suggested Marvely.

They found a place to sit in the lounge area. Chanice talked to a few people, and everybody seemed incredibly friendly. After about half an hour she began to feel light-headed.

"Whew, I think my ex is kicking in," said Marvely.

"I'm not sure, but I think mine is too," said Chanice. Did I say that? she thought. It sounded so strange. Then she giggled. Joanne and Marvely started giggling, too.

"Yeah, this is it!" Joanne said, excited.

Suddenly Chanice felt light as a feather, as if she were floating through the air. She also felt very happy, and everything around her looked beautiful. "This is a gorgeous club! The lights are so pretty," Chanice said.

"It is beautiful," said Marvely through clenched teeth, her voice shaky.

They all smiled at each other for a moment, then Joanne suggested dancing.

"Yes, let's dance!" Chanice shouted.

Chanice seemed to be drifting to the dance floor on a wave of pleasure, and she felt the music fill her. She danced as she'd never danced before, feeling the beat in

26 every part of her body. They danced for four hours. Then suddenly Chanice started getting tired. She was no longer feeling exhilarated, and she was very thirsty.

"We're comin' down," said Marvely.

"I need a drink and a seat," said Chanice.

Chanice was dizzy. After fumbling with her wallet at the bar, she got a drink and stumbled to the lounge. She was so dizzy she could barely walk. The three friends thumped down at a table. Suddenly Chanice felt her entire body fall. She wasn't floating anymore. I don't want this to end, she thought. I need more. I want to be happy and high again.

"Let's do more. Can we do more?" she begged her friends.

Marvely and Joanne looked at each other and laughed. "Do you realize it's 7:00 in the morning?" said Joanne.

"It can't be!" Chanice said. She was starting to ache all over, and her thoughts were getting jumbled. "I'm going to get more."

Joanne looked annoyed. "Okay, do what you want. But we can't stay. I have to go to bed," she said.

Drugs make it hard for you to focus on anything that needs concentration.

28   Chanice found the man in the baseball cap and gave him $100 for four capsules, then left the club with her friends. By now her ecstasy had completely worn off. She felt depressed and confused.

I just blew $100 on drugs, Chanice realized. But I want to feel that good again.

When Chanice returned home from New York, she found dealers who sold ecstasy around her school. Chanice started taking ecstasy every Saturday night and felt really high. But the more she did it, the more depressed she got in between. She became trapped in a miserable cycle of highs and lows. Chanice became dependent on ecstasy to bring her out of the depression, but each time she used ecstasy it left her even more depressed later, which made her crave ecstasy even more.

She couldn't focus on school. She alienated her friends, who couldn't understand why she was always sad and irritable. She spent more and more time alone. Finally, her father confronted her. He asked if she was using drugs. She denied it. But a week later, while buying ecstasy from a dealer, she was arrested. Chanice had let drugs rule her life.

The Dangers of Mescaline

Phil's family was visiting some relatives in Chicago for a few weeks. Being from a small town, Phil was nervous about hanging out with his cousin Max. He wanted to impress Max and convince him that he was cool. Max's friends seemed so much more with-it than the guys back home.

Max introduced Phil to a bunch of his friends, including a gorgeous girl named Delia. Phil felt awkward around Delia. He really wanted to impress her, but he didn't know how.

After hanging out with Max and his friends outside the minimart one day, Phil asked Max about Delia. "Hey, Max, does Delia have a boyfriend?"

"Nah—but she definitely doesn't have a problem getting a date. She's one of the most popular girls at school. There's usually a bunch of guys around her trying to get her attention. Why? You interested?" asked Max.

Phil shrugged, his cheeks turning red.

"Come on, man. Tell me the truth. Maybe I can help," said Max.

"I don't know—yeah, I guess I wouldn't mind going out with her," Phil replied shyly.

Appreciating the world's natural beauty is one way to feel great.

"Well, let's just say you've got a lot of competition. Take my advice and loosen up a little. Delia's always hanging with the cool guys from school. You need to act like you know what's up," said Max.

"How do I do that? She makes me nervous. I don't know what to say to her," admitted Phil.

"Listen, there's a party at Delia's place tonight. That's your opportunity to impress her. I have something that will help loosen you up," Max said.

Max pulled a plastic bag out of his pocket and took out a capsule.

"What's that?" asked Phil.

"It's mescaline. It'll help you relax. You'll see some really cool visions. By the time we get to the party, you'll be so relaxed and calm, you'll definitely impress Delia," said Max.

"I don't know. I don't really do drugs. Is this dangerous?" asked Phil.

"Nah—I've used this before. I got it from a friend of mine. He's Native American, and his tribe uses it during religious ceremonies. Come on, don't be a wuss. It's perfectly safe," said Max.

Phil still wasn't sure if it was a good idea. He had never used drugs before, and he knew that they were dangerous.

A true friend will try to help another who is on drugs.

But then he thought of Delia and how much he wanted to impress her. Besides, Max had taken it before, and nothing had happened to him. Phil reluctantly swallowed the pill.

By the time Phil and Max reached Delia's house, Phil was feeling queasy. Inside, the music was pounding, and everyone was dancing. The room was hot and filled with smoke. Phil began to feel dizzy and weak, and his head was aching.

Delia spotted the boys and started walking toward them. As she came closer, Phil noticed that she looked really odd. Her eyes seemed to glow red, and her skin was yellow. She leaned forward to kiss Phil on the cheek, but to him it looked like she was about to attack him.

With a shriek Phil spun around and tried to run. Suddenly everyone frightened him. They all looked like demons! One of them grabbed his arm.

"Phil, Phil! Snap out of it, man! You're just having a bad trip. Relax!" said Max as he tried to calm Phil down.

But Phil couldn't hear Max. All he saw was a demon shaking him.

Terrified, Phil ran out of the house. He wandered the streets, afraid of everything he saw. He spent a horrible night

34 | hiding from everyone.

When the police found Phil sleeping in the park the next morning, they brought him back to his cousin's house. Max had told Phil's mother what had happened, and she had called the police.

Phil promised himself that he would never do drugs again. He was sorry that he had worried his mother and made a fool of himself in front of Delia and everyone else at the party. But most of all, he never wanted to be that scared again.

Nikki Said Yes to Marijuana

Nikki and Robin were next-door neighbors and best friends. They went almost everywhere together. They even had the same birthday! Nikki was quiet and shy around people she didn't know well. Robin was more outgoing and made friends easily.

In their junior year, both girls turned seventeen and got their driver's licenses. The following weekend they went to a school basketball game. Nikki drove.

During the game Robin began talking to several older girls who were sitting by them. Mona, one of their new friends, invited Nikki and Robin to a party at her house after the game.

Nikki and Robin accepted. After all, what possibly could happen? Nikki had her parents' car for the evening. If the party was dull they would not even need to call home for a ride. They could just leave.

"Mona said the refreshments are big submarine sandwiches and beer," Robin told Nikki later as they drove to the party. "But I'm sure they'll have soft drinks, too."

"Don't be so sure," Nikki replied. "We don't know Mona that well. It's hard to guess what she and her friends may do."

"So we'll see," Robin answered. "If the party is in the fast lane, we'll just leave."

"Agreed!" Nikki replied.

When Nikki and Robin got to the party they were impressed. There were more boys than girls—for a change! And everyone seemed friendly.

"I'm Garth," said a cute guy standing by the refreshments. "Can I get you something to drink?"

"Do you have soda?" Robin asked. "Yes, what do you want in it?" Garth smiled.

"A few ice cubes would be great," Nikki replied. She picked up a paper plate and reached for a sandwich.

"We can do better than that!" Garth boasted. "How about a little vodka?"

36

"No, thanks," Robin replied.

"I'll pass, too," Nikki told Garth. She took the soda and balanced it on the edge of her plate while Robin got a sandwich. Then both girls looked around for a place to sit.

"Most of these guys are seniors," Robin said between sips of her soda. "I've seen them at school."

"Yeah," Nikki agreed. "And every one of them is cute!"

"Having a good time?" Mona asked as she weaved her way through the crowd.

"The sandwiches are delicious," Robin answered.

"This is Garth and Dino," Mona said. She casually introduced them to each other. "Have fun."

Garth sat down beside Nikki. Dino sat down on the other side of Robin. Garth talked about school and discussed his plans for college. Nikki was glad to listen. Then he asked her to dance.

Nikki was having a great time. Garth was a good dancer. After the first few minutes she did not even feel awkward. But she did get tired and needed to catch her breath. So they sat out the next few dances.

Teens often start smoking because of peer pressure.

38

Garth lit up a joint and offered Nikki a drag. "Want some grass?"

"No, thanks," Nikki said. "I tried pot once when I was about 12. It didn't do anything for me."

"Your grass probably didn't have much THC in it," Garth explained. He looked at the joint in his hand. "This stuff is super! Today's marijuana has more THC. It can really make you feel good!"

Garth put the joint up to Nikki's lips. "Go ahead," he urged. "Take a drag."

Nikki knew she should say no again. But she liked Garth. She hoped he would ask her for a date. She didn't want him to think she was a baby. Besides, she had tried pot before and nothing bad had happened.

So Nikki said yes and inhaled deeply. She held in the smoke as long as she could. Then she let it escape slowly from her lips. She felt like coughing, but instead she cleared her throat.

After Garth finished the joint, he and Nikki began dancing again.

Now Nikki felt as if she were walking through a dream. Everything Garth said seemed so funny that she could not stop giggling. She kept stepping on Garth's toes and giggling even more.

"My feet seem to have a mind of their own," Nikki said. "Are you sure you didn't spike my soda with alcohol?"

"It's the pot," Garth insisted. "It's making you feel slightly drunk."

"Umm," Nikki said. "I didn't think anyone could get *slightly* drunk."

When the record ended, Robin came over to Nikki. "We should leave now," she insisted. "It's getting late."

"Okay," Nikki said. "Goodbye, Garth."

"I'll call you, Nikki," Garth promised.

As they walked to the car Robin said, "Give me your car keys. I'll drive."

"Forget it," Nikki snapped back. "I'm perfectly capable of driving!"

"Look, Nikki," Robin said. "I saw you smoke pot. I know you're high. Your reflexes are so affected that you could hardly dance! Let me drive."

"We are only 10 blocks from home," Nikki pouted. "Nothing will happen."

Nikki got behind the wheel and started the car. As she pulled away from the curb she almost sideswiped several parked cars.

"Some people don't know how to park!" she complained to Robin. She did not say that the cars looked blurry and their shapes seemed to keep changing.

Drugs change the way you experience reality and make it very dangerous to do things that require good judgment.

"Please let me drive, Nikki," Robin
pleaded. "I'll be careful with your parents'
car."

"I can do it," Nikki insisted. "We'll be
there in a few minutes!"

Nikki tried to stop when they came to a
traffic light. But her foot could not find
the brake pedal. Nikki drove through the
red light.

They were hit by a car that started to
cross the intersection on the green light.

Brakes squealed. Cars twisted around
each other. Glass broke and flew. Blood
splattered. Bones were crushed. Cries of
pain were heard everywhere.

Robin ended up in the hospital with
seven broken ribs and several cuts and
bruises.

But Nikki was not so lucky. She was
dead on arrival at the hospital.

"Nikki should never have said yes to
marijuana," Robin moaned between sobs
to her parents. "Nikki was my friend...
she was a good person. She just made a
foolish mistake."

John Said Yes to LSD

John's introduction to heavy drugs came at
a very young age. He did LSD for the first

42 time when he was 16. He didn't know a lot about drugs; he thought it was cool to do drugs. He was in a band, and the band members would all trip together. They all thought it improved their music.

John was really enjoying the hallucinations and the energy, just having fun with it. He had no idea you could have a *bad* trip. That is, until it actually happened.

It was a Saturday night at around 12:30 a.m. The band members were hanging out in the practice room. They had each taken a hit of acid about an hour ago, and it still had not kicked in. George, the lead singer, suggested that they take more. John was bored, so he agreed. But as soon as they swallowed the second hit, the first one took effect—and it came on strong.

It was the strongest stuff John had ever done. He was nervous. *One* hit was almost too much to take. How was he going to deal with two?

The more he thought about it, the more panicked he became. He suddenly started sweating and felt sick to his stomach. He thought everyone was out to get him and was afraid talk to any of his bandmates. He just didn't trust them; they

seemed scary. They saw that John was
freaking out and tried to help, but the
more they talked to him, the more frightening they seemed.

Bill, the drummer, suggested that if John
ate something it might help him come
down. He gave John a slice of white bread
and a glass of orange soda. John managed
to unclench his jaw and shoved a piece of
the bread between his shaking lips. He
didn't realize how dry his mouth had
become—there was almost no saliva in it.
The bread stuck in his throat. He tried to
wash it down with the soda, which tasted
like sugar and bitter chemicals.

Soon he felt the nervous rush of the
second hit washing over him, sweeping
him even further away from reality. John
feared that he had gone completely insane
and would never come back. He couldn't
see anything. Everything was just a blur
of color.

John was disoriented. He had lost all
concept of time. At one point it seemed to
him that things were happening over and
over again. The same song seemed to be
playing on the radio for hours, when it
actually only played once. Everything kept
"looping" that way, again and again. All he
wanted was for this nightmare to end, but

44 he was tripping so hard it seemed to last forever.

John knew a lot of people who always took acid at Grateful Dead concerts. They had talked about the love and harmony everybody shared while high on the drug. So why was he so afraid? He was terrified of his friends. He thought they were plotting against him, and he knew he had to get away from them before they hurt him. When he finally managed to get to his feet, he stumbled to the bathroom and locked the door. He sat in the bathtub in total darkness for the rest of the night, waiting for the terror to subside.

John woke up the next morning incredibly sore and unable to think clearly. He snuck out of the house, too embarrassed to say good-bye to his sleeping bandmates. When he got home, he realized he must look awful, because his mother gave him a funny look.

"Rough night?" she asked, putting groceries away.

John's brain searched for a response, but he couldn't think of anything. Rough night? What did she know? Was she playing some weird mind game? He couldn't answer. His mother put down her groceries and stared at him, concerned.

When drug users become addicts, they often turn to crime to support their habits.

46 Why couldn't he answer her? "Stop looking at me!" he thought.

"We stayed up late practicing," John finally blurted out. Fortunately, she didn't push it, and John escaped to his bedroom and slept for the rest of the day.

John wished someone had warned him that LSD use could cause him to have terrifying experiences like the one he had. He promised himself that he would not say yes to drugs again.

Molly Said Yes to PCP

Both of Molly's parents had to work long hours. Molly was often at home alone. When she was younger, she played outside with other kids in the neighborhood. But now she spent more time alone. She was usually inside watching TV or doing homework.

Molly's older brother, Marco, was 17. Marco often stayed out late or he did not come home at all. On weekends he and his friends usually drank beer and did drugs on the back porch.

Marco usually stayed away from Molly, but when she turned 12, Marco gave her a drag off his PCP joint as a birthday present.

Molly became very excited and started
acting crazy. She climbed onto the swing
that hung from a tree and started doing
dangerous stunts. Molly fell off the swing
many times and scraped her arms and knees.
But she did not feel any pain, so she let
her wounds bleed and kept showing off.

After that, Molly joined her brother and
his friends when they smoked joints laced
with PCP. Soon she became hooked.

Molly began having trouble at school.
She could not think straight or remember
things. She often got mad at her teachers
and was very rude. Her classmates also
got on her nerves. Molly would push them
out of the way when she walked down the
halls. Everyone began to avoid Molly.

The school principal sent a letter to
Molly's parents requesting a conference,
and her mother was furious.

"Are you in some kind of trouble?" she
asked, showing Molly the letter.

"No," Molly replied. "It's just that the
teachers don't like me. They're on my case
for nothing!"

Molly's mother asked a school counselor
to have a phone conference since she could
not get time off from work.

"The counselor told Mother that you are
moody and rude and failing most of your

Sudden failing grades are sometimes a sign of drug use.

classes," Molly's father reported. "You're grounded until you straighten this out!"

Grounded? Molly almost laughed. She did not have any friends to run around with anymore. They had all dropped her. And she did not care. When she was not smoking PCP with Marco and his buddies, she slept. So what if she was grounded?

Molly knew she should lay off the drugs for a while and pay more attention to her schoolwork. But it was too late. She could not get through the week without her PCP at least every other day.

Molly was not quite 13, and she was sick of always being on the wrong side of the rules. First at school, and now at home. Maybe she needed help. Maybe she should tell her mom. But her dad would kill her if he knew she did drugs!

One weekend Marco and his friends and Molly were high on PCP. The boys began arguing about getting money for more drugs. They punched each other around. One of them pulled a knife and cut Marco on the arm. They complained that Molly did not do her share to bring in money. Then they told her that they were going to rob a gas station at midnight and she had to come along.

50

"I didn't know you broke the law to buy drugs," Molly told Marco. "Why didn't you tell me before?"

"Don't worry, Molly. I'll take care of it," Marco insisted. "I don't want you to get involved in this."

"But I am involved!" Molly pouted. "I want to help!"

Molly was sent into the gas station to buy a bag of chips. She was pretty nervous, and she felt a little dizzy. But she was fearless. She felt as if she could handle the robbery all by herself if necessary.

When Molly went to the check out, the manager rang up her purchase. While the cash register was open, Marco and two of his friends burst through the door and demanded money.

The station manager set off an alarm, and the noise sent Marco into a rage. Marco started spraying the room with bullets. He yelled something, but his words were slurred. Molly could not tell if he was talking to her or trying to scare the manager. Marco shot the manager just as the manager drew a pistol and shot Marco.

"Come on," the boys shouted at Molly as they ran out the door. "Leave him!"

Small crimes, like stealing from home, often lead drug users to larger crimes that support their growing habit.

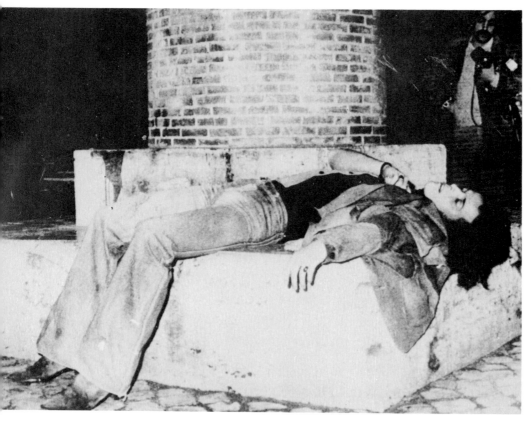

Many drug users lose control of their lives.

But Molly was horrified. She could not leave her brother dying on the floor. She bent down and held Marco's head in her lap. She kept calling his name. When the police arrived they had to pull a screaming Molly away from her dead brother.

Molly's father later told her that she had been fingerprinted and had spent the night in jail. But Molly did not remember any of it. The last thing she remembered was the look in Marco's eyes when he went into that rage.

Molly even blocked out most of the time she spent in the hospital and later in the halfway house. Because of her age, Molly was not sent to prison, but she now had a criminal record.

By the time Molly straightened out her problems with the law she was 14. And she felt rotten. Because she was still on probation, she had to live at home. And she had to go to school. Molly was so depressed that she wanted to stop living.

Marco was dead. His friends were in prison. Molly felt guilty, too. She had no friends of her own. Her parents blamed her for Marco's death, and they did not talk to her. Big deal! They were never home anyway! Now the only person Molly ever saw was her parole officer.

Molly hated her life. She slept through most of her classes. When she did stay awake, she got into trouble with other students or with her teachers. She spent more time waiting outside the principal's office than she did in the classroom.

Molly simply couldn't cope with her life without drugs.

54   But she needed money to buy drugs. So Molly began selling her body to get money for drugs. She knew that sleeping around was as dangerous as doing drugs. But by now she did not care. She had absolutely no self-respect. Her self-image could not have been lower if she had pulled the gun and shot Marco herself.

Molly looked up some of Marco's old friends. They sold her drugs. When they could not get PCP, she bought whatever they had. They often sold her ecstasy, which they claimed was even better than PCP. She did not care what she used as long as it kept her from thinking about her problems and her life.

Molly soon overdosed. Was it on purpose? Or did the drugs she bought poison her?

Molly was 14 when she died. She had used PCP for two years and other drugs for about three months. She did not want to say yes again to drugs. But she did not have the courage to say no.

Molly was so confused that she did not even try to get help. She could have gone to a clinic or a hospital for therapy to help kick her drug habit. She could have asked for help at school. She could have asked her parents to help her. Her friends might have kept her from feeling so lonely, if she had had any friends.

But Molly could not think clearly. She could not see an end to the mess her life had become. Molly became one of a huge number of people who die from using drugs every year.

Molly let drugs destroy her life.

Parents, teachers, friends, and counselors are just a few of the
people who can help teens work out their problems.

CHAPTER 3

Asking for Help

*Y*ou have now read about the dangers of hallucinogens and some stories of what has happened to those who used drugs. Although the stories presented in this book are fictional, they are based on reality. The dangers of hallucinogens and other drugs are real, and the lives of many young people have been destroyed by these drugs.

It's impossible to predict how a drug will affect a person. Every person's experience is different. Even if you have a friend who tells you that he or she has taken the drug and nothing bad has happened, there is no guarantee that you will have the same experience.

It is also important to realize that heavy or prolonged use of a hallucinogen

58 | can cause brain damage and mental illness by killing brain cells.

No matter what anyone tells you, hallucinogens are not safe. You have no way of knowing what is actually in the drug you buy. Most drug dealers mix other substances into the drugs to increase the amount they can sell.

If you have a problem with hallucinogens or other drugs, there are people who can help you. There are many teens who have managed to overcome their problems with drugs because they asked for help. If you know you have a problem, talk to someone. Turn to a friend, a relative, or a teacher and ask them for help.

At the back of this book, there is a list of organizations that can also help. Most of these have counselors who have been trained to help people deal with drug problems. If you want to find an organization in your town or even if you just want someone to speak with, call these places. They can help you or refer you to counselors in your area.

Drugs do not have to control your life. Reach out for help, and you can learn to live a drug-free life.

Glossary

amphetamine Drug that speeds up the
functions of the brain and body.

hallucinogen Drug that upsets the
chemicals in the brain, causing the
user to see, hear, smell, and behave
differently.

high The effects of a hallucinogen on the
user.

hooked State of being addicted to a drug.

LSD *Lysergic acid diethylamide*, a strong
human-made hallucinogenic drug.

MDMA Human-made hallucinogenic
drug, also called *ecstasy*, that contains
a mix of both LSD and amphetamines;
very popular at raves.

"magic mushroom" Mushroom
(fungus) containing *psilocybin*, a
hallucinogen.

60 **marijuana** Most commonly-used illegal drug in America; often causes mild hallucinations and mood changes.

mescaline Natural chemical that is a hallucinogen; found in the peyote cactus plant.

overdose Too much of a drug, causing sickness or death.

PCP *Phencyclidine*, the most dangerous human-made hallucinogen.

peyote Cactus plant whose top "button" contains *mescaline*, a hallucinogenic drug.

psilocybin Natural chemical that is a hallucinogenic drug; found in "magic mushrooms."

rave All-night underground party at which ravers dance to techno music and often take ecstasy or Special K.

Special K *Ketamine hydrochloride*, a popular drug at raves that acts like both hallucinogens and amphetamines; legally used by veterinarians as an animal tranquilizer.

THC *Tetrahydrocannabinol*, a common hallucinogenic chemical found in marijuana.

tripper A person who has upset the chemicals in his or her brain by using a drug.

Where to Go for Help

In the United States

American Council for
   Drug Education
164 West 74th Street
New York, NY 10023
(800) 488-DRUG

The Hazelden Foundation
C03, P.O. Box 11
Center City, MN 55012
(800) 257-7810 (in U.S.)
(651) 257-4010 (outside
   U.S.)

National Clearinghouse for
   Alcohol and Drug
   Information
P.O. Box 2345
Rockville, MD 20847-2345
(800) 729-6686
Web site: http://www.
   health.org

National Council on
   Alcoholism and Drug
   Dependency
12 West 21st Street,
   7th Floor
New York, NY 10010
(800) NCA-CALL
Web site: http://www.
   ncadd.org

Nar-Anon Family Group
   Headquarters, Inc.
P.O. Box 2562
Palos Verdes Peninsula,
   CA 90274
(310) 547-5800

National Drug and Alco-
   hol Treatment Referral
   Routing Service
(800) 662-HELP

In Canada

Alcohol and Drug Depen-
   dency Information and
   Counseling Services
   (ADDICS)
#2, 2471 1/2 Portage Ave.
Winnipeg, MB R3J 0N6
(204) 831-1999

Family Services Youth
   Detox Program
4305 St. Catherine's St.
Vancouver, BC V5V 4M4
(604) 872-4349

Narcotics Anonymous
P.O. Box 7500
Depot A
Toronto, ON M5W 1P9
(416) 691-9519

For Further Reading

Algeo, Philippa. *Acid and Hallucinogens.* New York: Franklin Watts, 1990.

Anonymous. *Go Ask Alice.* New York: Simon & Schuster, 1971.

Ball, Jacqueline A. *Everything You Need to Know About Drug Abuse.* Rev. ed. New York: Rosen Publishing Group, 1998.

Berger, Gilda. *Addiction.* New York: Franklin Watts, 1992.

Johnson, Gwen, and Bea O'Donnell Rawls. *Drugs and Where to Turn.* New York: Rosen Publishing Group, 1993.

Sexias, Judith. *Drugs: What They Are and What They Do.* New York: William Morrow and Co., 1991.

Shulman, Jeffrey. *Focus on Hallucinogens.* Brookfield, CT: Twenty-First Century Books, Millbrook Press, 1991.

Index

About the Authors

Ann Ricki Hurwitz holds a BA in linguistics from the University of Colorado. Sue Hurwitz holds a MA in education from the University of Missouri. They are coauthors of eighteen short stories and a social studies textbook for young adults.

Photo Credits

Cover photo: Stuart Rabinowitz
Photos on pp. 2, 17, 20, 22, 27, 32, 48, 51, 56: Dru Nadler;
p. 8: Photo Researchers, Inc. © Allan D. Cruickshank;
pp. 13, 37, 40: Stuart Rabinowitz; p. 30: Mary Lauzon;
pp. 45, 52: AP/Wide World.

Design: Blackbirch Graphics, Inc.